The Odds Strike Back!

Adam Perrott

Illustrated by
Tom McLaughlin

LITTLE TIGER
LONDON

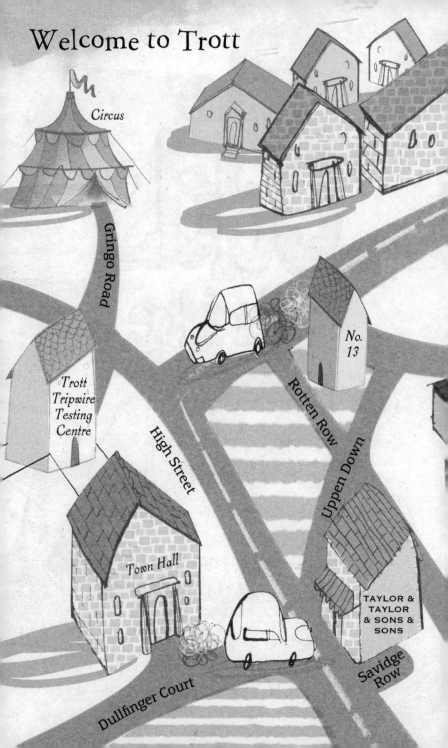

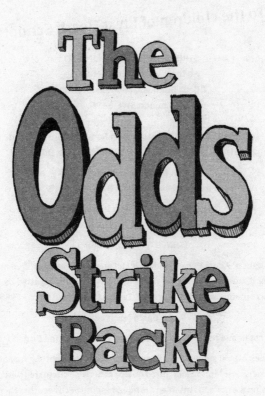

The Odds Strike Back!

For Joanne ~ AP

To the children of Clyst Heath School ~ TM

STRIPES PUBLISHING LIMITED
An imprint of Little Tiger Group
1 Coda Studios, 189 Munster Road,
London SW6 6AW

Imported into the EEA by Penguin Random House Ireland,
Morrison Chambers, 32 Nassau Street, Dublin D02 YH68

A paperback original
First published in Great Britain in 2013

Text copyright © Adam Perrott, 2013
Illustrations copyright © Tom McLaughlin, 2013

ISBN: 978-1-84715-368-5

Printed and bound in the UK.

The Forest Stewardship Council® (FSC®) is a global, not-for-profit organization
dedicated to the promotion of responsible forest management worldwide.
FSC® defines standards based on agreed principles for responsible forest
stewardship that are supported by environmental, social, and economic
stakeholders. To learn more, visit www.fsc.org

2 4 6 8 10 9 7 5 3

Snootypants Manor

Church

Choffingly Way

Pillingly Drive

Aardvark Avenue

Bibbleswicke Gardens

St Mump's School

The Swankington

Chapter One

BAD NEWS FOR THE ODDS

It was a merry old day in the town of Trott and a typical breakfast scene at number 13 Rotten Row, the home of the Odds. Mr Odd was in the kitchen frying toadstools, Mrs Odd was dangling from the light fittings by her ankles and their twins – Edgar and Elsie – were riding around on the back of a pair of extremely warty warthogs. It wasn't your average breakfast, but then the Odds are not really your average family.

For those of you unfamiliar with the Odds, the family is (in descending order):

 Mr Odd...

 Mrs Odd...

Edgar Odd...

Elsie Odd...

And Bob (the Odds' dog).

They are all Meddlers, otherwise known as Professional Pranksters, and it's their job to cause as much mischief as they can every day without getting caught. Just like a teacher's job is to shout and give out homework. Or a businessman's job is to be a man that does business.

Mr Odd is an expert Stuff-Hiderer and Thing-Mover. He could hide a great white whale in a blackboard shop and still you wouldn't find it until it sprayed you in the face with its blow-hole.

Mrs Odd is a messy Mischief-Maker who loves to make mess. Her favourite pranks usually involve kitchens and excessive amounts of flour, or milk, or eggs. Or custard. The end result often resembles a giant pancake. With custard.

The Odd twins, Edgar and Elsie, love scary pranks and hearing their victims shriek in terror is as joymongous as a volcano filled with jellybeans destroying your school.

And Bob, the Odds' dog, is a retired Meddler's pooch who was an active meddler in his day, but now enjoys the quiet life. After all, dogs age faster than Meddlers, and Bob has earned a good rest.

"You two!" Mr Odd bellowed at Edgar and Elsie, sticking his head round the kitchen door. "Stop that at once. Those pet warthogs aren't even filthy! Take 'em out into the back garden and get some mud on their trotters this minute!"

The twins galloped out of the back door.

"You're a good dad, my sweaty little spit valve," said Mrs Odd, giving her husband a crinkly wink.

"Thank you, my little maggot-chewer," Mr Odd replied, giving his wife a wrinkly crink. "It's not easy raising children correctly."

"I know what you mean," Mrs Odd nodded grimly, "but we've got ourselves a right pair of rotters there, no mistake."

Mr and Mrs Odd looked out at the twins, who were now wrestling in the mud with their warthogs. They beamed like two proud beetroots when, at that moment, there was a knock on the door.

"That knock sounded rather post-like," said Mr Odd. "I bet it's the postmeddler."

Mrs Odd answered the door (slipping in warthog dung as she went). Sure enough, there was Mr Pratt the postmeddler standing on the doorstep.

"Good mornin', Mrs Odd," said Mr Pratt. "I've got some lovely post for you!" He handed her three envelopes, two of them white and one of them bright red. "That one needs signing for, if you please," said Mr Pratt, pointing to the large red envelope and handing Mrs Odd a clipboard with some paper attached. "Oh, and here's *The Meddlers' Post*," he added, handing her a grubby and smudged newspaper.

"Thank you, Mr Pratt," said Mrs Odd, wiping a large piece of snot on the paper and two small bogies. "This red letter looks very important."

"It's sealed with the Prime Meddler's crest," said Mr Pratt, pointing to the earwax seal on the back of the envelope on which was stamped the profile of the Prime Meddler himself. "I wonder what it might be?"

"I can't wait to find out," said Mrs Odd, shutting the door in the nosy postmeddler's face.

"Anything good, my slippery watervole?" said Mr Odd, dishing up his fried toadstools on to the breakfast plates as he opened up *The Meddlers' Post*. "I wonder if there's any news about the Plopwells in here? Ah yes, here we are...

PRANKING IMPOSTORS
IMPRISONED

Meddling miscreants Mr and Mrs Strange were sentenced yesterday to twenty-seven and a half years de-Meddlification for breaking Meddling

Law. The Stranges, disguised as rich twits the Plopwells, embarked on an elaborate plot to oust another Meddling family, the Odds of Rotten Row, Trott, from their home. This grave crime directly contradicts one of Meddling society's strictest laws as written down in *The Meddlers' Mischief Manual* – Don't nick from other nickers. As such, Mr and Mrs Strange are banned from any sort of Meddling activities and will be fitted with Anti-Meddling Manacles until their sentence is served in full.

"Wow," said Mrs Odd. "Twenty-seven and a half years with no meddling. But they don't even mention it was us what stopped 'em!"

"They don't, do they? The rotten rapscallions," said Mr Odd, scratching his head and watching as three woodlice and a millipede fell out and had a race to the end of the breakfast table.

"The cheek of it!" said Mrs Odd. "We stop the meddling crime of the century and we don't even get the credit. And what about poor old Bob?" She gave their mongrel's flea-riddled head a scratch under the table. "Forgotten about, as usual."

"Who's Bob?" said Mr Odd. "Only jokin'! Who could forget about ol' Bob? The best meddling mutt a Meddler could ask for. But let us all remember, we don't meddle because it might make us famous, or rich but because it's our duty as Meddlers to cause chaos and make mischief wherever there is order and calm."

"Well said, my untidy turnip," said Mrs Odd, taking the paper and looking at the front page.

THE MEDDLERS' POST

COUNCIL OF PRANKIFICATION ELECT NEW HEAD PRANKER

"Ooh, fancy that," said Mrs Odd to Mr Odd. "The Council of Prankification have elected a new Head Pranker."

The Council of Prankification are in charge of what goes on in the Meddling World. They are a greasy, sleazy, cheesy and slimy bunch of crooked old crab-faces who shouldn't be trusted with a box of cotton wool, let alone the welfare of a species.

"Who is it?" asked Mr Odd.

"It's Nobody," Mrs Odd replied.

"Oh," sniffed Mr Odd. "That's strange – why would they elect nobody? Seems like a waste of time to me, and not very newsworthy to boot!"

"No," said Mrs Odd, "it's Nobody."

"I heard you the first time," Mr Odd replied, "and my views remain the same on the subject. I can't see how electing nobody into a position of power is a worthwhile step."

"NO!" Mrs Odd was getting rather angry now. "They've. Elected. NOBODY!"

"It doesn't matter how many times you say it, my shrivelled little fig, I still say it's a useless headline. It's like saying: EVERYTHING'S FINE or NOTHING HAPPENED TODAY, REALLY, HOW ARE YOU? Complete waste of time..."

Mrs Odd grabbed Mr Odd by the scruff of his scruffy jacket and shook him.

"NO! LOOK!" She thrust the newspaper in his face. "READ. THE. ARTICLE!"

Mr Odd ran his beady little eyes over the beady little words till the story formed in his brain.

"Oh," he said when he'd finally finished, "they've elected Nobody – as in *Mr* Nobody – as the new Head Pranker. But the Head Pranker is second only to the Prime Meddler, who is second to nobody. Not *Mr* Nobody, just nobody."

"Exactly." Mrs Odd raised her eyebrows.

"Wait a snot-dribbling minute!" Mr Odd leaped to his feet, knocking over his chair in the process. "I've just remembered I HATE Mr Nobody! I've ALWAYS hated Mr Nobody! I hate Mr Nobody more than I hate taking baths, or sliding down banisters. Wait a minute – I LOVE sliding down banisters, but I still HATE Mr Nobody!"

"I know you hate Mr Nobody, dear," said Mrs Odd. "But please, don't tell us the story of how you and Mr Nobody—"

But it was too late. Mr Odd had started. "It was approximately twenty-four years, nine months, three weeks and four days ago last Wednesday," he said, his eyes glazing over. "Mr Nobody and I were Meddling partners, the best in the business. We could prank anyone, anywhere and anytime. Except on Tuesday evenings, when we were at our badminton club. We were both at the top of our game – I'm talking about pranking now, not badminton, you understand."

"Yes, dear, I know," said Mrs Odd, clearly exasperated that Mr Odd was telling this story ... AGAIN!

"Good. We were the best there was ... I'm still talking about pranking."

"I know, dear."

"We would smash that shuttlecock from Meddleton town centre to Slackville Multistorey Hedgehog Aquarium and back again like there was no tomorrow."

"Now you're talking about badminton!"

"I'm talking about pranking! Pay attention! Who even said anything about badminton? Anyway, after our weekly badminton game, we would each cadge a lift on the back of a passing vulture and make our way home. But one fateful night, fate had other fateful plans in his fatey underpants' pockets. Because walking towards us, was the then Prime Meddler herself, Mrs Petunia Peculiar."

"Not the Mrs Petunia Peculiar?" asked Elsie, as she and Edgar trotted in on their substantially-muddier-than-they-were-earlier warthogs.

"Yes, Elsie, the Mrs Petunia Peculiar. And well done, that warthog is substantially muddier than it was earlier."

"Did you talk to her?" asked Edgar.

"Of course I did, Edgar," Mr Odd replied. "The story of what happened next is a tale of woe..."

"Yeah," Elsie muttered, "as in whoa don't tell us again."

"I heard that!" Mr Odd snapped. "Anyway, where was I? Oh yes, well, we scraped together a right mouldy old dustbin lid full of rotten kippers, banana skins, potato peelings, lemming snot and a decomposing mango and we was all set for pranking Mrs Peculiar. Oh, we were so excited about pulling such a rot-tastic prank, *and* on the Prime Meddler herself, but unbeknownst to me, ol' Nobby Nobody had another idea. We leaped out at her and Nobody was meant to chuck the contents of our mucky dustbin lid over her, when all of a sudden Nobby chucked it right over me instead – in my mush!"

Mrs Odd, Edgar, Elsie and Bob and the two substantially muddier-than-earlier warthogs all stifled giggles. Even though they'd heard the story before, it was still funny.

"Oh, you think it's funny, do yer?" Mr Odd bellowed. "Well, I'll tell you why it wasn't. Right, it wasn't funny for three reasons. One, we was supposed to be partners in prankery and instead he turned on me like a little Tommy Turncoat. And two, it took me ages to get all that decomposing mango out of my hairy left nostril."

"Er, that's two, Dad," said Edgar, who was good at counting.

"Oh." Mr Odd sneezed two centipedes and a dung beetle out of his hairy left nostril. "There and then," Mr Odd continued, "Mrs Peculiar was so impressed, she made Nobby Official-Tea-Boy-in-Charge-of-Making-Coffee-and-Other-Hot-Beverages at the Council of Prankification. He must have worked his way up to become the new Head Pranker. It should've been me ... then I could be sitting in a big fancy office all day eating teabags and drinking sandwiches and stealing staplers..."

"But you've never wanted to be the Head Pranker," Mrs Odd pointed out.

"And we still love you, Dad," said Edgar.

"Yeah, you'll always be the best pranker in our house," said Elsie.

"Not just our house," said Mrs Odd. "In Meddleton, if not the whole world!"

The two warthogs grunted in a reassuring way.

Mr Odd sniffed. "But I ain't got one of them big fancy spinning chairs you get in an office, though, have I?"

"Well," said Mrs Odd, "we can always sit you in one of our normal chairs and whizz you around. That might be fun?"

"Come on now, Odds," said Mr Odd dejectedly. "I'm not going to make you lot whizz me round on a chair. You'll do yourselves an injury." He looked a bit sad.

"Are you all right, my evil toad-lobber?"

asked Mrs Odd, stroking Mr Odd's hair, then shaking her hands free of nits.

"I'll be fine, my little tube of toothpaste," said Mr Odd. "It's just some bad news, that's all. Oh well, at least I won't get any more today. No, sir. No more bad news for the Odds for a good long while. Why, we may never get any more bad news ever again, I shouldn't wonder."

Just then, Mr Odd noticed the bright red envelope with the Prime Meddler's crest on the back.

"Oooh," he said excitedly, picking it up. "I wonder what this is..."

Chapter Two

EVEN MORE BAD NEWS FOR THE ODDS

"Oh no..." said Mr Odd, his little black eyes skimming the page. "It's an inspection! The Council of Prankification want to do an inspection!"

"Who do they want to inspect?" asked Elsie.

"Us, of course!" said Edgar. "Right?"

Mr Odd nodded.

"When are they coming?" said Mrs Odd.

"It's OK." Mr Odd breathed a sigh of relief. "It's this Wednesday."

"This Wednesday?" The other Odds looked at each other.

"Er... Dad?" said Edgar. "It *is* this Wednesday. Today is Wednesday."

Mr Odd smiled at Edgar. "Oh, my little simple son. It says right here that we are due to be inspected this Wednesday – OH, GREAT HAIRY NETTLE TOADS, IT'S TODAY!"

"They can't inspect us on the day we get the letter telling us we're being inspected!" said Mrs Odd, peering at the envelope. "Look at that! They haven't put enough postage on, it's a week late! Who does it say is inspecting us?"

Mr Odd went, if possible, even paler than usual. "Mr Nobody ... Mr Nobody's arriving any time now to inspect us!" said Mr Odd. "And seven plus three = ten!" he added. "He hates me and he'll fail us no matter what! But wait ... it's OK," Mr Odd smiled, "it says here it's at nine am. We've got loads of time."

"Er... Dad?" said Elsie. "It's quarter to nine."

"Oh, Elsie," Mr Odd laughed, "my little daft

daughter... Quarter to NINE!"

"Exactly," said Edgar. "What are we going to do?"

"I don't know!" Mr Odd screeched back. He turned to his wife. "Maybe we should do a spot of panicking, dear, what do you think?"

Mrs Odd slapped Mr Odd round the face with a haddock. "Now, let's calm down and think about this, my handsome parsnip-gobbler," she said kindly.

"What is Mr Nobody coming round here to inspect us for exactly, Dad?" asked Elsie.

"Everything." Mr Odd slumped back down in his rotten old chair. "It's a Head Pranker's job to make sure every Professional Prankster is pranking as professionally as they can. It's a tricky thing, keeping up this level of professionality..."

"Ism," said Mrs Odd.

"Sorry – professionalityism. But I reckons what ol' Nobby's really got in mind is to come sniffing around my house to see what I'm up to. I bet he's the first Head Pranker in a month of Thursdays who's personally inspected a Meddler's house. They normally get their snivelling little lackeys to do it instead and report back. I reckon Nobby just wants to gloat at me because he's Head Pranker and I'm stuck here."

A stony silence followed.

Then a rocky quietness.

A pebbly calm drifted in.

Followed by a gravelly stillness.

"So what do you think Mr Nobody will check

for while he's here?" asked Elsie.

"That we're keeping up with our pranks," said Mr Odd, "and thinking up new ones all the time, finding new victims, annoying the same ones. He'll also want a rundown of all our best pranks of the last few years."

"Well, that's easy," said Edgar, "we pranked the Plopwells good and proper, didn't we?"

"That's right," said Elsie. "Pranked 'em like a pair of kippers!"

"You're right," said Mr Odd, "but that won't impress ol' Nobby Nobody. We need more. We should come up with a plan. A spectacular plan. A snumptastic, rumpy-bogsticks sort of a plan to show his Head Prankership what I ... I mean we ... are capable of. Who's got one then?"

The Odds looked at each other for some time.

Then they looked at Bob.

Bob looked at the inside of his eyelids. He was asleep.

"I dunno, Dad," said Edgar. "It's really hard to keep thinking up plans all the time."

"Especially good ones that work," said Elsie.

"Ah, my two little Trainee Tricksters." Mr Odd sat down next to his children and put a bony arm round each of them. "Thinking and planning is what a Meddler does best. Thinking up a prank, planning it out and then..." He rubbed his hands together. Then he stopped. A look had crept on to his face, a look that the rest of the Odds knew only too well. He was getting an idea. A snumptastic and rumpy-bogsticks sort of idea. "Wait a minute..." he said, his eyebrows raised like two giant, hairy caterpillars. "Wait a tiny, shiny, shiver-down-me-spiny minute here... I've got the perfectest prankiest weep-into-a-hankiest pranking plan I've ever had in all my life..."

"What is it?" shouted the rest of the Odds – all except for Bob, who said nothing (he was still asleep).

"When ol' Nobby walks through our front door," Mr Odd stood up and began pacing as he did whenever a pranking plan plopped into his brain, "we prank him in exactly the same way he pranked me all those years ago – just as soon as his feet touch the carpet! We'll pull the finest prank this side of Pranksylvania!"

"You mean chuck rotten food all over him?" said Mrs Odd, leaping out of her chair. "What a great idea! Just brilliant, my little guava stuffed with fresh mildew!"

"It's fantastic, Dad," cried Edgar. "He won't know what's hit him! Unless he can remember what happened nearly twenty-five years ago, but even if he can, he won't like it!"

"Quite right, Edgar, and there's not a moment to lose." Mr Odd started commanding his troops. "Go outside and get the biggest dustbin lid we own. Elsie, you go outside and find one even bigger than the one Edgar finds and meet back in the living room."

The twins rushed outside and came back a few seconds later, each with a dustbin lid exactly the same size.

"Right," said Mr Odd, who was now as giddy as a giddyfowl on holiday, "we start filling the dustbin lids."

"With what, my slippery carbuncle?" asked Mrs Odd.

Mr Odd looked serious. He looked his wife straight in the eye so there could be no misunderstanding about the words he was going to say. "Mrs Odd. Fetch the biggest jar of Festering Putridness we have..."

The other Odds gasped.

"Are you sure?" said Mrs Odd.

"As sure as I am sitting here," said Mr Odd,

quickly sitting down.

Festering Putridness is truly horrible stuff. It could be found in every Meddling household from here to Bunktonbridge Cat Farm. It comes in various shapes and sizes, but the ingredients are always the same. Namely the most foul and disgusting contents from the foulest and disgustingest places in the world, all brought together in the same handy jar.

FESTERING
PUTRIDNESS

Ingredients:
• Aged mucus (twelve
months at least)
• Discarded scabs
• Hedgehog droppings
• Cold rat-sick
• Pus-filled boils from an
ostrich's leg
• Runny rotten egg yolks
And much more

"Festering Putridness, Dad..." said Edgar, hardly able to contain his glee. "I've been waiting to use Festering Putridness my whole life. That'll give ol' Nobody-pants the pranking of a lifetime!"

The Odds leaped to work. As Edgar and Elsie had both brought in dustbin lids of the same size, Mr Odd decided to use Elsie's and save Edgar's for back-up, in case they ran out of room on the first one. Mrs Odd dragged in the jumbo family pack of Festering Putridness from under the kitchen sink.

"Right," said Mr Odd, opening the jar as the Odds gathered round for this momentous occasion. "Everybody dig — " He stopped, then looked at his family. "It's completely and utterly empty, save for half a black banana skin and a small rotten cockroach leg!" he said.

"What?" Mrs Odd peered inside. "It can't be... It was a brand-new jar. Someone's been pilfering!"

"Well, it wasn't me!" said Mr Odd.

"It wasn't me!" said Edgar.

"It certainly wasn't me!" said Mrs Odd.

Suddenly it dawned on them like ... dawn. All eyes turned to Elsie, whose own eyes were looking at the floor.

"Have you got anything to say, little Miss Mudskipper?" said Mrs Odd, her hands on her hips.

Elsie slowly looked up at them all. "I'm really sorry," she bleated like a sad sorry sheep. "I was going to replace it."

"Oh really, young lady McFaydy," said Mr Odd. "And what, pray tell, did you want with all that beautiful Festering Putridness?"

"I wasn't doing anything wrong, honest!" screeched Elsie. "I just took it and stuffed it down the pipe organ's pipes in church, that's all."

"Whatever for?" asked Edgar, a little forlorn that his sister had clearly been on a prank without him.

"Because ... because ... horrible old Mrs McSimmons is getting remarried in a few weeks' time and I thought we could all watch as the organist plays the organ and ... splat..." Elsie tailed off.

"Poor old Mrs McSimmons," Mr Odd chuckled. "Who is she anyway? And why does she deserve our *entire* batch of Festering Putridness?"

"Mrs McSimmons," said Elsie, "is the worst human being in the ENTIRE world. She's one of our school dinner ladies and is a total and complete bag of wrong."

"What does she do that's so bad?" asked Mrs Odd.

"Things like..." Elsie cast her mind back, "dishing out tiny portions of the good stuff – pizza, or cake, or fish fingers – but splashing out great walloping dollops of mushy peas, broccoli and spinach. Or saying that she hasn't got chips when I know she has."

"That doesn't sound too bad, my wee unhappy flannel," said Mr Odd. "In fact, it sounds like she'd make a good Meddler."

"No, she wouldn't!" snapped Elsie. "Meddlers are hardworking Professional Pranksters. She's just a rotten trout-mouth who's so bad, mean and downright nasty that her getting covered in Festering Putridness shot from a pipe organ on her wedding day is her getting off lightly."

"Oh, my darling little doorstep-stepper," said Mrs Odd soothingly. "It doesn't matter that you took the Festering Putridness now that we know your intentions were good."

"Yes, my tiny bottle of giant squid ink," said

Mr Odd, "your mum's right, but it doesn't change the fact we've got no Festering Putridness left now and Mr Nobody's about to arrive!"

Mrs Odd sat down, suddenly looking rather worried. "We could go out and find some more..."

"There'll be no time for that, my little tea-strainer!" said Mr Odd. "Mr Nobody could be here any minute, giving us orders, flicking his earwax at us..." Mr Odd suddenly looked quite sad. "I suppose we could think up another prank altogether, but I did so have my little beating heart set on that one."

Mrs Odd eyed Mr Odd nervously, as though she was about to tell him something that would make him leap out of his chair, scuttle up the curtains and perch on the curtain rail.

"Well," she said. "We could always call for ... Granny Snott...?"

Mr Odd leaped out of his chair, scuttled up the curtains and perched on the curtain rail.

Chapter Three

GRANNY SNOTT

"Not now, not never, not no way!" Mr Odd squealed like a naughty budgie. "I'm not having that busybody old bat of a badger-basher in my house. EVER!"

"But she's our only hope of getting any more Festering Putridness," said Mrs Odd, her eyes widening like saucers.

"Yeah, Dad," said Edgar and Elsie, their eyes staying relatively the same size, like teaspoons.

"I don't care!" Mr Odd blustered. "I can't stand

that know-it-all Nelly Noodle-Noggin and no mistake."

"But she is my mother, my sneaky charm-bucket," said Mrs Odd.

"How could I forget?" said Mr Odd, still perched on the curtain rail. "Every Christmas and birthday card she's ever sent me reminds me that I'm not good enough for you and that she hates my face."

"Oh, that's nonsense," said Mrs Odd.

"Is it?" Mr Odd leaped down from the curtain rail and landed neatly in a plant pot. "Well, take a look at these then!" He produced from one of his many voluminous pockets a pile of old and rather tattered cards. "I keep them on me at all times in case I should ever have to use them in an argument. Look, let's read one at random, shall we? Here we are!" Mr Odd opened one out. "'To my son-in-law...'"

"Well, that doesn't sound so bad," said Mrs Odd.

"I was just taking a big enough breath! 'To my son-in-law ... who I hate with all the passion of a thousand fiery suns exploding into one colossal supernova, leaving in its wake the Earth and all the other planets of the Milky Way as mere floating balls of dust and ash unfit to carry life upon them ever again... Season's Greetings.'"

"OK, so that one's a particularly bad one," said Mrs Odd.

"That's the best one!" said Mr Odd. "And the only one I could read out in front of the children!"

"Well, what do you suggest?" said Mrs Odd. "We don't have any Festering Putridness and Mr Nobody could be here any minute."

"But I don't want her in this house!" snapped Mr Odd. "She's a menace. I just won't have it."

"Aw, go on, please! We haven't seen Granny in ages!" moaned Edgar.

"Let us see her, Dad!" groaned Elsie.

"Come on, let us call for her, my little flop-weasel," cooed Mrs Odd.

Mr Odd ummed and ahhed, and ummed some more like an ummingbird and an ahhing board mixed together until, with a sigh, he said. "NO! I hates her!"

Then he ummed and ahhed some more until at last he finally said, "NO! NO! NO! NO! NO!"

Then Mrs Odd and the twins got fed up and called her anyway. They stood in a line, each winked once with their left eye, flexed the big toe on their right foot three times, jumped in a circle, touched their noses and cried, "GRANNY SNOTT! GRANNY SNOTT! COME AND SHOW US WHAT

YOU'VE GOT!"

Suddenly, from out of thin air, there came a rip-roarious explosion, the sound of screeching car tyres and a cat yowling like it's just had its tail trapped in a geography teacher's pen drawer.

When the smoke had settled (there was smoke, too), there stood, in the middle of the Odds' living room, a short, wrinkly woman wearing an old tartan dress, a purple fez with a black tassel, yellow-and-pink polka-dotted wellington boots and an eye-patch. She was standing behind a huge wooden cart on two wheels that was filled to the brim with every possible pranking aid ever invented by Meddlers.

Granny Snott is what is known in the meddling world as a Pedlar Meddler. Whenever a Meddler finds themselves in a fix, or finds they've run out of earwigs, or itching powder, or super-sticky glue made from the tentacles of the Giant Sucking Squid of Borneo, they call on a Pedlar Meddler to drop by.

"Well 'ello, me little tinkers!" she bellowed, flapping over to Edgar and Elsie and giving them huge hugs and kisses. "Them atomic boosters got me here quick, didn't they?" she said, pointing to a pair of what looked like rockets that were attached to the bottom of the cart.

"Hello Gran," said Elsie, beaming.

"Hello Gran," said Edgar, also beaming.

"What a pair of beamers!" said Granny Snott. "Now go and 'elp yerselves to whatever yer want from me cart."

Edgar and Elsie both rushed over to Granny Snott's cart and began rooting around for some terrible treats. "And 'ello, my little antique horseshoe!" she said, hugging Mrs Odd tightly. "How are things?"

"Not too bad, Mother," said Mrs Odd nervously, "not too bad."

"Good good," said Granny Snott, turning to Mr Odd. "And you... How are you, you who I hate with all the passion of a thousand fiery suns exploding into one colossal supernova—"

"Yes, yes, we've already been through all that," Mr Odd bit back. "Rest assured, Granny Snott, I didn't want you here either. We're just in a little bit of a pickle, that's all."

"Oh, really?" Granny Snott grinned. "And what kind of pickle are we in?"

Mrs Odd explained all that had happened –– from the letter, to finding out that Elsie had used the last of the Festering Putridness down the pipe organ's pipes to shower Mrs McSimmons at her upcoming wedding. When Mrs Odd had finished, Granny Snott was well and truly caught up with the events.

"Well, well, well..." Granny Snott tutted and began pacing around in her yellow-and-pink polka-dotted wellies. "What a pickly pickle you've pickled for yourself this time, pickle-face."

"Oh, shut yer trap."

"Mr Odd!" Mrs Odd screamed. "Don't talk to my mother like that!"

"Sorry," said Edgar sheepishly. "It was actually me. I've been working on my Dad impression for weeks now."

"Well, practise it another time," said Mrs Odd.

"It was rather good, though, wasn't it?"

"Really good," said the real Mr Odd in his real voice, looking proudly at his son, "and accurate, too – shut yer trap! See?"

"Do you want my Festering Putridness or not?" Granny Snott shrieked like a banshee with a degree in Shriekery.

"I've got all the Festering Putridness I need just looking at you!" Mr Odd shrieked back like a banshee with a masters degree in Advanced Shriekery.

"That doesn't even make sense!" Granny Snott retorted.

"I know it doesn't!" Mr Odd conceded. "And nor do you! Just fill this dustbin lid, will you, before Mr Nobody knocks on our d–"

KNOCK! KNOCK! KNOCK!

"Oh no!" Mr Odd squealed. "He's here! And my fabulous prank is nowhere near ready!"

"Sorry..." said Elsie this time, knocking three

times on Granny Snott's cart. "I've been working on my knocking-on-a-door impression for weeks now. Between us, me and Edgar can make it sound like Dad's talking and knocking on a door when really he's not."

"Oh, Elsie, not now!" said Mrs Odd, though both she and Mr Odd were very proud of their little pranksters. "Look, Mother, why don't you–"

KNOCK! KNOCK! KNOCK!

"Elsie!" said Mrs Odd. "I said 'not now!'"

"That wasn't me, Mum," said Elsie, stuffing a bag of large earwax cubes that looked just like blocks of fudge into her pocket. You never know when they might come in handy...

"Then who was it?" asked Mr Odd, his beady eyes sweating beads of beady sweat.

"It was I!" came a grand voice from behind the door that sounded like the person thought he was more important than he actually was. "Mr Nobody. I'm here for my inspection!"

"Quick!" Mr Odd hissed like a snake in a library. "Fill this up!"

Granny Snott filled the dustbin lid full of Festering Putridness until it was overflowing. As quick as a slippery wink, Mr Odd opened the door a fraction before scuttering and skittling up the wall and carefully balancing the dustbin lid on top of the door and then bunkling back down to ground level.

"Come in, Mr Nobody, sir!" Mr Odd bellowed, sniggering under his breath. "Come in and don't look up whatever you do!"

The Odds held their breath as the door opened and in walked, or rather in rolled, Mr Nobody in his ever-so-fancy big leather office chair with wheels, behind his ever-so-fancy big office desk (also on wheels) with pens on it and everything. He had a moustache and was wearing a very swanky pinstripe suit with a red bow tie. He was being pushed by a short, round little Meddler who wore a dull, grey suit with a mustard-yellow tie.

"All be upstanding," said the Meddler pushing Mr Nobody's desk, "for the Head Pranker himself – Mr Nobody!"

Everyone stayed exactly where they were.

"I'm his personal assistant, Mr Crawley..." he continued.

Still nobody moved, or spoke.

They were too busy watching Mr Odd's spectacular prank unfold.

The Odds held their breath as the dustbin lid teetered and tottered, then tittered then tuttered until finally it tattered and fell...

Right on Mr Odd's head, covering him in recently acquired Festering Putridness and knocking him out cold.

Chapter Four

"Er, that wasn't meant to happen, was it?" said Edgar.

"HA!" Granny Snott barked like a triumphant walrus who'd just won a free trip to the circus for himself and three other walrus friends. "What a popple-hooped hobbler! Pranked by his own prank!"

"Oh no," hissed Elsie. "Dad's pranged his own bonce instead of Mr Nobody's."

"He must have got the angle wrong," said

Edgar. "Or miscalculated the force with which Mr Nobody opened the door. After all, Meddling can be a very exact science."

"I take it that prank was meant for me, was it?" said Mr Nobody, filing his nails. "The same prank from twenty-five years ago. Pathetic. But then again, I was always in a different class to you, wasn't I, Mr Odd?"

"Are you all right, Dad?" Edgar leaned over Mr Odd as the other Odds gathered round.

Mr Odd didn't stir. He was knocked out colder than an icicle in a penguin's playground.

Then, a moment later, Mr Odd blinked twice and sat up straight. He looked at Mrs Odd, Edgar and Elsie, then at Granny Snott, Mr Nobody and Mr Crawley.

"Who are you all then?" he asked, wearing a bewildered smile. "Partridges."

The other Odds looked at each other. Then at themselves, just in case they weren't who they thought that they thought they were.

"It's us, Dad," said Edgar.

"Edgar and Elsie," said Elsie. "Your two little snot-ripplers."

Mr Odd looked at them both and smiled. "Nice to meet you, Alfred and Gertie." He stood up and shook them by their ankles. "How do you do? And you are?"

"I'm Mrs Odd," said Mrs Odd. "I'm your wife?"

Mr Odd looked at her closely. "My...?"

"Your wife!" shrieked Mrs Odd. "You must remember, surely!"

"Ah, of course," beamed Mr Odd. "Nice to meet you, Shirley. Now, who am I? Bagpipes."

"What's wrong with Dad?" asked Edgar.

"That bang on the noggin musta sent him doo-la-de-daa-down-dippy," said Elsie.

"He's gone and forgotten who we are," said Mrs Odd. "And he's gone and forgotten who he is, too! And he's inserting random words at the end of his sentences!"

"I find that very difficult to believe," said Mr Nobody.

"No, it's true," said Edgar. "Go on, Dad, say something else."

"Who, me?" said Mr Odd. "Like what? Hexagon."

"See!" said Elsie.

"Well, once again I disagree," said Mr Nobody. "It is my belief that Mr Odd is trying to play a prank on me, and if there is one thing I know, it's never stick your face in a bowl of jam, then head-butt a wasp's nest. But if there's another thing I know, it's never trust a pranker."

"Very true, oh great Head Pranker," said Mr Crawley. "Very true indeed."

"Thank you, Crawley," said Mr Nobody. "Now be quiet, and don't open your mouth again until I tell you to, but only if I'm speaking in a very, very high-pitched voice. Understand?"

"Yes, oh wondrously Tricksy Trubster."

"I didn't say it in a very, very high-pitched voice!" Mr Nobody replied, in a very, very averagely pitched voice. "Understand?" he continued in a very, very high-pitched voice.

"Understood, my Hoax-a-licious Host, oh Grand-High Meddler, oh Swindlerific One!" said Mr Crawley.

"All right, enough of this nonsense!" said Granny Snott, barging forward and kicking Mr Nobody and Mr Crawley out of the way with her yellow-and-pink polka-dotted wellingtons. "I'm getting sick of you two! Right, here's how we tell if he's really pranking you or not." She marched up to Mr Odd and dragged him to his feet by his hairy left nostril. "Hello, you lizard-lipped ferret-faced sea-slug-sucking excuse for a dog's dinner! You remember me, don't you?"

Mr Odd stared at Granny Snott.

Granny Snott stared back.

"You must remember me, you scrawny-boned baboon-bottomed earwig-breath?" Granny Snott tried again.

Mrs Odd, Edgar and Elsie all took a step backwards. Mr Odd and Granny Snott's arguments were legendary. Once, they had argued for so long Mrs Odd and the twins had gone on holiday for a fortnight and arrived home to find them still arguing.

"Sorry," said Mr Odd, holding out his hand, "how do you do? My name is ... sorry, I don't seem to recall. Do you know it? Is it Lizard-lipped ferret-brained sea-slug-faced excuse for a dog's dinner? Or perhaps it's Scrawny-boned baboon-bottomed earwig-breath? I don't mind either, though they're both a bit long – the initials wouldn't fit on my hankies."

The whole room stood, aghast.

Then they sat, aghast.

Finally they lay down, aghast, before getting up again, aghast.

"He's got concussion," said Granny Snott.

"We need to get him to a hospital!" said Mrs Odd. "Quick, everyone, pack up all his belongings – his chair, his favourite magnet and his collection of rusty muskets."

"I don't think so," said a drawly voice. Mr Nobody scootled up to the Odds. "I'm here to inspect you all, and inspect you all I shall."

"But he's not well in the head," said Granny Snott. "Even more so than usual, I mean."

"Thank you very much. Piffle," said Mr Odd.

"You can't very well inspect my family's pranking skills when my husband's not in any state to be pranking!" said Mrs Odd.

"Indeed I can, Madam," said Mr Nobody, "and indeed I will. I shall get my personal private physician and doctor, and amazing inventor, Dr Klampit, to come at once."

"Dr Klampit?" said Elsie. "The same Dr Klampit who invented Dr Klampit's Al-harm Clock?"

"And Dr Klampit's Three-Bounce Bouncing

57

Boom Balls?" said Edgar.

"The very same," said Mr Nobody smugly. "I'm going to phone him right now. He'll soon be able to tell us if there's something wrong with Mr Odd or if, as I suspect, he is faker than Freddy Fake of Fakingham Crescent."

"Too true," said Mr Odd. "Pogo."

Chapter Five

Twenty minutes later, Dr Klampit screeched to a halt outside the Odds' house and knocked on the door.

"Sorry I'm late," he said as he flapped in through the cat flap, white coat billowing heroically like a cape, and his medical diploma (in a mahogany frame) underneath his arm. He was a short Meddler, completely bald except for his ears so hairy you could house badgers in them. "What seems to be the trouble?"

"Wow! Dr Klampit's here in our house!" said Edgar.

"I can't believe it!" said Elsie. "We're big fans."

"I love your Screeching Beans," said Edgar.

"I love the Sticky Zip," said Elsie. "I get Edgar with it all the time!"

"She once swapped all the normal zips on my trousers with Sticky Zips!" laughed Edgar. "I couldn't fasten my flies all day! I got her back, though, with one of your tubes of Troothpaste! One quick morning brush and she was spilling secrets all over the breakfast table!"

"Well, I'm glad to hear my marvellous Meddling inventions are keeping a generation of Trainee Tricksters on their toes," said Dr Klampit with a smile. "So where's this patient you called me about, Mr Nobody?"

"Right here, Doctor," said Mr Nobody.

"He needs brain medicine!" screeched Mrs Odd.

"Nonsense!" said Granny Snott. "He just needs to drink some of Granny Snott's Good Ol'

Fashioned Mashed Cauliflower, Seaweed and Lugworm Tonic. Cures everything. Probably. Might kill 'im, though. Let's just give it a go and see, eh?"

"No!" said Edgar. "He needs a really, really good shake!"

"No!" said Elsie. "He needs a really, really good sneeze!"

"No!" said Dr Klampit. "If he sneezes, he'll sneeze his brain out through his nostrils! Trust me, I'm a doctor."

"Brain medicine!" screeched Mrs Odd.

"Tonic!" squealed Granny Snott.

"Shake!" shrieked Edgar.

"Sneeze!" wailed Elsie.

"Rawr!" rawred Bob. Which meant: "A concussion has no quick-fix cure. Treatment of concussion involves monitoring and rest. Symptoms usually go away entirely within two weeks, though they may persist or complications may occur."

"What?" said Dr Klampit.

"He said, 'A concussion has no quick-fix cure. Treatment of concussion involves monitoring and rest. Symptoms usually go away entirely within two weeks, though they may persist or complications may occur,'" repeated Elsie.

"That's what I thought he said," said Dr Klampit. "But he is a dog and I am a doctor, so you will excuse me if I don't take the word of a mangy old mutt over my mangy old doctory expertise. Now, Mr Odd." Dr Klampit stood before Mr Odd and put his stethoscope on Mr Odd's head, "say hmmmmm..."

"Hmmmmm..." said Mr Odd.

"Now say Oooooo..."

"Oooooo..." said Mr Odd.

"Good," said Doctor Klampit. "Now say both of them one after the other."

"Hmmmm ... ooooooo..." said Mr Odd.

"It's bad, I'm afraid," said Dr Klampit. "He clearly thinks he's a cow."

"What can we do, Doctor?" said Mrs Odd.

"My poor little rattlesnake can't even remember his own name! Or what species he is."

"There's nothing we can do, my good woman," said Dr Klampit, packing his stethoscope away. "Like the dog said, things should be back to normal in about two weeks or so."

"Two weeks, eh?" Mr Nobody chimed in.

"That's right," said Elsie suspiciously. "Why?"

"Well, I'll tell you why, my dear, and the why is for this: two weeks is exactly how long I was planning on inspecting you for!"

"Two weeks!" the Odds bellowed as one.

"But that's a terribly long time!" said Mrs Odd. "And for us not to have our best pranker!"

The other Odds all nodded and mumbled in agreement.

"Nevertheless," said Mr Nobody, "that is how it is. I shall be moving my office into your house and watching your every meddling move, from your individual pranking abilities to your achievements as a family."

"We pranked the Stranges!" said Edgar.

"They were disguised as normal people, but we saw straight through them. They were trying to get us out of our house, but—"

"I don't care about your past achievements, boy," said Mr Nobody. "I care about these next two weeks. Because if you don't impress me, then you may well find yourselves sharing the Stranges' fate..."

The Odds gasped.

Mr Nobody smirked.

Mr Crawley chuckled.

"Bandicoot," said Mr Odd.

Chapter Six

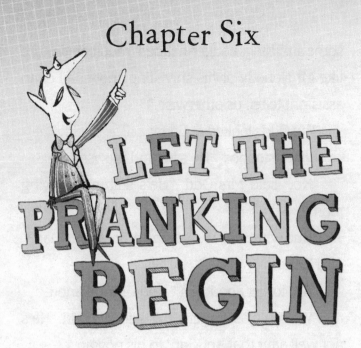

LET THE PRANKING BEGIN

Mrs Odd, the twins and Granny Snott had all crept into the kitchen while Mr Nobody and Mr Crawley had a Who's-Got-the-Most-Evil-Smirk-or-Chuckle Competition, and Mr Odd watched invisible dandelions dance around his head.

"What are we going to do?" Elsie hissed.

"We do what we always do, Elsie," said Mrs Odd. "We prank our little pranking brains out."

"Business as usual," said Edgar. "With or without Dad. We're the Odds. We don't need some smirking, badger-headed, mop-eared murp like Mr Nobody or his snivelling snot-snail of an assistant to tell us otherwise."

The Odds looked at Edgar.

Edgar stopped. "He's behind me, isn't he..."

"No," said Mrs Odd. "He's still in the living room."

"But what are we going to do about Dad?" said Elsie.

"Ah, forget about 'im," said Granny Snott.

"We can't just forget him!" said Mrs Odd. "He's not well after that knockin' to his noggin."

"He's no use to us right now, though. We can't have him joining in and spoiling this inspection," said Granny Snott. "He'll bring you all down."

"We'll just have to keep him out of Mr Nobody's way," said Mrs Odd. "Granny Snott will help us prank, won't you?"

Granny Snott looked at Mrs Odd for some time. "Oh, all right then. If I must."

"But what about your cart and your business selling stuff to other Meddlers?" said Edgar.

"You and Elsie can look after it," said Granny Snott. "I trust you with it."

Edgar and Elsie looked at one another like all their Christmases and birthdays had come at once and they were really, really good ones with pogo-sticks and roller-skates and sugar-coated jelly mice.

"Do you mean it, Gran?" said Elsie.

"Honest?" said Edgar.

"Of course," said Granny Snott. "Like I said, I trust you. To cause as much mischief as you can!"

Edgar and Elsie laughed.

"OK," said Mrs Odd, "so we just get on with things as normal. Business as usual."

"Business as usual, eh?" came the drivelly voice of Mr Nobody as he rolled into the kitchen. "That's good to hear."

"Are you going to start inspecting us right now?" said Mrs Odd.

"I'll have you know, my dear woman," said Mr Nobody, "that I have been inspecting you from the moment I wheeled through your door. I've been inspecting everything about you. From the state of the grime underneath your fingernails, to the happiness levels of the mildew in your bathroom. Actually, my inspection began even before I arrived. Yes, I am so thorough I even inspected the pavement on the way to your house, the doorstep and the very door I knocked on, in case it failed to meet regulation door-knocking thickness and minimum knuckle-resistance."

"How did we do?" asked Elsie.

"So far, perfect," said Mr Nobody grudgingly.

"But don't get too excited – very few Meddlers fail an inspection at the door-knocking stage. Now, I think it's time I saw you all at work..."

"Now?" cried Mrs Odd.

"Yes, now," said Mr Nobody.

"Well we're not ready to be inspected!" said Mrs Odd. "We're not prepared!"

"That's the whole point of the inspection," said Mr Crawley. "To see you as you normally go about your pranking duties."

"That is correct," said Mr Nobody, unfurling a large blackboard from his desk drawer and standing it beside him. "I have here a list of the things you will be inspected on."

The Odds looked at the list, their jaws dropping.

"There're hundreds of things on there," said Mrs Odd.

"Four hundred and seventy-eight, to be precise," said Mr Nobody, smiling.

"Number thirty-nine," said Edgar, reading aloud, "keeping one's composure whilst being

71

chased by a goat? How are you meant to do that?"

Mr Nobody's eyes narrowed.

"Number two hundred and one," read Elsie, "sneakery."

"Fairly self-explanatory, I'd say," said Mr Nobody.

"What's three hundred and fifty-nine all about then?" said Edgar. "Lemon drops and a new hoover bag?"

"Ah," Mr Nobody leaped from his chair and wiped number three hundred and fifty-nine off his blackboard. "I remembered some shopping I had to do as I was writing this list."

"You can go and do it now, if you like," said Granny Snott. Then, turning to Mrs Odd, she mumbled, "Wait till he's out of the house, then we'll pack up and leg it. I hear Outer Mongolia's pretty nice this time of year."

"Oh, I don't think so, Granny Snott," said Mr Nobody. "I don't need to do my shopping just now. I shall be buying all the lemon drops and hoover bags I desire just as soon as I have failed ... I mean, inspected you and your family. I think I shall start with ... you two..." He pointed his fancy pointing pen at Edgar and Elsie.

"Oh, sponge crumpets," moaned Edgar.

"With frog jam and eel spit," moaned Elsie.

So Edgar and Elsie found themselves being followed on their way to school by Mr Nobody. Mr Crawley scuttled along behind his boss, all the while taking care to avoid the dog muck, lamp posts, lamp-post muck and dog posts.

Edgar and Elsie arrived at St Mumps and walked through the gates as normal while Mr Nobody and Mr Crawley snuck in through a manhole and hid in an old grandfather clock in the main corridor.

"What are we going to do?" asked Edgar.

"I don't know," Elsie replied. "We're just going to have to prank like we've never pranked before."

"But won't that make things worse?" said Edgar, as confused as a man with his balaclava on backwards. "If we prank like we've never pranked before, then we'll have never pranked before and so we won't know anything about pranking and it'll all go horribly wrong!"

"It's just an expression, Edgar," said Elsie

harshly. "And I know you've heard of it before –
everyone has – so stop being stupid."

"Sorry," said Edgar. "I am a bit annoying at
times, aren't I?"

"I'll say," said Elsie.

"You'll say what?" said Edgar, proving his
earlier point.

"Just save it for ol' Nobby, will you? We need
to do this right, especially with Dad the way he is."

That morning, after the regulation fire drill, bomb
drill, dentist drill and stampeding porcupine drill,
the Headmistress of St Mumps, Mrs Missus, called
an emergency assembly.

"As you may all or may not all not know," she
began, rather confusingly, "today is school sports
day."

"We didn't know that, Miss!" said Andrew
Missus, Mrs Missus's second nephew four times
removed.

"You never told us, Miss," said his brother.

"I haven't brought me kit, Miss," his second cousin piped up.

"Well, I don't care," said Mrs Missus. "Today is sports day so I want every last one of you outside – NOW!"

The whole school trudged outside on to the muddy playing field.

"The first event," Mrs Missus barked through a megaphone, "is the ... running race. Run from 'ere to there. GO!"

"We have to get pulling some pranks ... and fast!" said Elsie, as the first class began to run.

"What about if we replace all the eggs for the egg-and-spoon race with crocodile eggs?" said an eager Edgar.

"No!" said an unenthusiastic Elsie. "We've done that before. We need to do much better than that. Mr Nobody's watching us from that muddy puddle." She pointed to a large puddle of mud nearby where a pair of beady Meddler's eyes and a beady Meddler's snorkel were just breaking the surface. "We need to deliver our best prank to date. We can't keep swapping normal eggs for crocodile ones. People will say we've got predictable."

"I knew you'd say that!" said Edgar.

"I knew you'd say that!" Elsie quipped. "Now just use your brain for a minute, will you? And please try and think of something better than crocodile eggs!"

Edgar thought for a moment.

"... Alligator eggs...?"

"Now that's predictable!" said Elsie. "But wait! I've got an idea – look at those kids stood all in a line."

"Looks like they're about to race. What about them?"

"Just watch..."

Elsie slipped off like a spy sneaking out of spy school and crept over to the children waiting in line. Meddlers can move very sneakily when they want to.

"There," said Elsie, sneaking back a few moments later. "Edgar? Edgar, where are you?"

"Here!" gasped Edgar, appearing at her side. "I just had to nip inside for something. What did you do?"

"I tied all their laces together," Elsie sniggered.

"Brilliant!" Edgar sniggered back.

"Right!" bellowed Mrs Missus. "Enough of the running race. Everybody get ready for the three-legged race! We don't have any rope or anything, so you'll all just have to tie your shoelaces together. Oh look at that, you already have!"

"Oh slanderous canker-prongs!" cursed Elsie. "I haven't pranked them, I've helped them out!"

"Never mind, Sis," said Edgar sympathetically.

At that moment, there came a series of small explosions from the other end of the field. Everyone turned to see a group of high-jumpers being flung high into the air, much higher than any person could normally jump.

Edgar started to giggle. "I put tiny bits of Dr Klampit's Exploding Shuttle Putty on the soles of the high-jumpers' trainers. I won't be surprised if they break a few world records. And the sound barrier. And Earth's orbit."

"Tut-tut-tut," tutted Mr Nobody, tuttingly, writing things down on his clipboard. "Not a very good start for the Odd twins, is it? Exploding Shuttle Putty? How boring. No doubt you'll have made some of those high-jumpers famous. And tying shoelaces together? How very predictable. I hope your dear parents fare better than you two did..."

Chapter Seven

THE SWANKINGTON PRANK

The next day, Mr Nobody and Mr Crawley followed Mrs Odd out on her pranking spree.

Being an expert Meddler like Mrs Odd is a carefree and jolly experience. Your time is your own, you can be as hardworking, or as lazy as you like. One day you might be tackling epic pranks, like swapping every book in a library for copies of *The Non-Adventures of Ian Smith, The Most Boring Boy in the World That Nothing Exciting Ever Happens to Ever, Not Even at the End as a Surprise*. Or you might feel like a quiet day hanging around outside a café, simply flicking bogies into uncovered coffee cups. But when you're being followed by the new Head Pranker and his creepy assistant Crawley, it's not so easy to be spontaneous. It's more annoying than itching powder in your underpants during a sitting-still contest, having those two follow you around. Fortunately for Mrs Odd, Granny Snott had come with her for moral support.

"Do you think Mr Odd'll be all right at home on his own?" said Mrs Odd.

"I hope not," Granny Snott replied. "With any luck, he'll trip over a tripwire, fall head first into the toilet, and get flushed down the sewers where a believed-to-be-extinct race of prehistoric cave-crocodiles will beat him to death with discarded hockey sticks."

"That seems unlikely," said Mrs Odd.

"Well, one can hope," said Granny Snott, putting away her receipt from the Trott Tripwire Testing Centre Giftshop in her bag and taking out a book entitled, *Believed-to-be Extinct Races of Cave-Reptile, Their Homes, Habits and Sporting Weapons of Choice*.

"I left him reciting all the kings of Norway backwards," said Mrs Odd. "He was on Haakon VII (1872-1957) when I left."

"So was he anywhere near the toilet at all...?"

"No!" Mrs Odd said crossly.

"OK ... OK, no need to get snarkers! Now, what have you got in mind for today? Gotta be something big, something outrageous, something mind-blowingly fripplistic that'll impress ol' Nobby-bonce."

"I've been a Professional Prankster for years, Granny Snott, I think I know what I'm doing by now," Mrs Odd huffed.

"So you must have something that you've been waiting to pull out of the bag for a special occasion like this?"

"Well..." Mrs Odd smiled. "There is one thing."

"What is it?"

"Today is the grand opening of the

Swankington, Trott's newest and most swankalicious hotel." Mrs Odd rubbed her hands together. "In about an hour's time, there'll be a big street parade with marching elephants and dancers and giant party poppers. The Mayor of Trott himself is going to cut the ceremonial ribbon. I thought I would give him an awfully big prank."

"Sounds great," said Granny Snott. "Where do we start?"

"Underground, of

course…" Mrs Odd winked.

"Underground?" Granny Snott echoed.

"Follow me." Mrs Odd lifted up a manhole cover and slipped into the sewers. Granny Snott followed, a confused look on her face. "Is ol' Nobby still following us?" asked Mrs Odd, without looking round.

"Yes," Granny Snott hissed, stealing a quick glance behind her to see Mr Nobody skulking along the sewer tunnel, followed, as ever, by Mr Crawley.

"When I was a young Meddler girl," Mrs Odd began, "I would spend many a happy hour gallivanting around the sewers, skimming stones, dodging mutant alligators and training rats."

"Training rats?" said Granny Snott. "I had no idea."

"No one did," Mrs Odd smiled. "It was my secret project. I trained dozens of them to do all sorts of things – sit up, beg, jump up and down, impersonate historical military leaders of the past. That sort of thing. I was going to have the world's first all-rat circus. Like a flea circus, except that the fleas were on the rats."

"But you moved to Trott when you got married to old Frog-face," said Granny Snott. "What makes you think your rats will be down here in this sewer?"

"Because I trained them with this," said Mrs Odd, pulling out a small dog whistle that hung on a chain round her neck. "I told them all that one day, one special day, I might need them

86

again. They spread out far and wide, passing my message on. It's been a while, but there should be at least one or two of my former performers knocking around."

Mrs Odd blew the whistle. Not a sound came out – at least not one that a human or Meddler ear could hear.

"Nothing's happening," said Granny Snott.

"Just wait a minute," said Mrs Odd. "I know it's been a long time, but at least one dear old rattikins should remember the sound."

They waited.

And waited.

And waited.

Then they stopped waiting.

Then they had to start waiting again because nothing was happening.

Mrs Odd was just about to give up when her Meddler ears twitched.

"Listen!" she hissed. "Did you hear that?"

Granny Snott swizzled her ears around. "I didn't hear anything."

Mrs Odd swozzled her ears a bit more. "Yes, I can definitely hear something. It's far off, but getting closer. Almost like the rushing of water, or drums in the distance, or..."

"Millions and millions of rats racing towards us?" said Granny Snott, who was looking ahead through a big bent brass telescope.

"Yes, that's it – WHAT?" Mrs Odd shrieked.

"Up ahead!" Granny Snott yelped. "Rats! Millions and millions of flea-bitten plague-munchers!"

Then Mrs Odd saw them.

Rats.

Hairy ones, bald ones, fat ones and skinny ones, black rats and white rats, large rats and mini rats, all of them racing as fast as their ratty legs could carry them. They swarmed all over the tunnel floor, some even scampering up the wall like a dirty flood.

"I never thought there could be so many," said Granny Snott, a little bit worried she might be swept away in a sea of rats.

"There was never this many before," said Mrs Odd. "They must have multiplied like..."

"Rabbits," said Granny Snott.

"Rats," said Mrs Odd.

"Do you think they'll remember you?" said Granny Snott, eyeing the approaching rats that were nearly upon them with her good eye.

"Erm..." Mrs Odd began. But she needn't have worried. One of the rats stopped at Mrs Odd's feet, reared up on its hind legs and smartly saluted her with its little left paw.

"That's a 'yes' then," said Granny Snott. "Now what do we do?"

Mrs Odd grinned. "To the Swankington Hotel!"

Meanwhile, the big street parade was well underway. Elephants marched in time to the music played by the World-Famous Trott Marching Band. Inside the Swankington Hotel, the Manager – Mrs Clanger-Lang – was busy preparing everything before the first ever guests arrived.

"Now, everyone pay attention!" she shouted to the hotel staff, who were hustling and bustling around. "Everything must go completely perfectly for our grand opening, do you understand? The rules are here for all of you to see."

They turned and looked at the rules, even though they had all been forced to commit **them** to memory. Twice.

"Right, places, everyone!" Mrs Clanger-Lang screamed. "The Mayor is here, the Mayor is here!"

THE RULES FOR GUESTS AND EMPLOYEES OF THE SWANKINGTON HOTEL

1. No pets. Not even cute ones.

2. No Children. Not even pet ones.

3. Any guest or employee found wearing dirty or unfashionable clothes will be asked to leave immediately. Then brought back in again. Then thrown out.

4. No dust mites allowed.

5. Any pest of any kind found in this establishment will be shot from a cannon.

At that moment, the Mayor of Trott trotted inside the Swankington, nodding and smiling at the hotel employees as he did.

"Well, Mrs Clanger-Lang," he smiled, "what a lovely hotel you've got. I must say, I cannot wait to stay here. But first, let me meet all your hardworking employees – AAAAIIIEEEEEE! Is that a rat on Reception?"

Mrs Clanger-Lang spun round. There, for everyone to see, was a great hairy rat, sitting on

the front desk, writing in the big book of guests.
What it was writing, we will never know. Nor
will we ever know where it got its fancy, red,
perfectly fitting bellboy's hat from because at
that moment, Mrs Clanger-Lang flew into an
almighty rage and threw the nearest object to
hand at the rodent – an employee called Dennis.
Poor Dennis sailed beautifully over the Reception
desk.

"FETCH THE CANNON!" Mrs Clanger-Lang shrieked. "GET THAT RAT OUT OF HERE!"

"Which one?" said an employee named Trudy. "That one? What about that one, Mrs Clanger-Lang? Or that one. Or those twelve?"

Mrs Clanger-Lang turned round and went white with fear and red with rage, leaving her a very normal-looking pink colour. Several other rats were dotted around the hotel, four in the aquarium, seven in a pot plant and about twelve or so riding around on a luggage trolley.

From high up on the grand chandelier, Mrs Odd and Granny Snott giggled with glee.

"I think her head's going to explode," said Granny Snott.

"You just wait..." Mrs Odd blew three short, sharp blasts on her whistle.

Like a tidal wave, the millions and millions of trained circus rats suddenly exploded from every nook and cranny in the Swankington Hotel. They swept over every surface, clambered up every wall and terrorized every employee.

Mrs Clanger-Lang appeared to go into a state of shock. She just stood there, rigid and unmoving, as the rats overran the hotel. The Mayor screamed and started running around in circles like a noisy merry-go-round. He also made the mistake of opening the door to escape. The rats flooded after him, chasing him right up on to one of the marching elephants, which reared and trumpeted loudly before galloping off down the street, the Mayor clinging on for dear life.

The chaos outside as every man, woman, band-member and elephant tried to escape from the horde of rats did a Meddler's heart proud. As the last of the rats filed out of the Swankington (sweeping Mrs Clanger-Lang and the rest of the workers out with them), Mrs Odd and Granny Snott leaped down from the chandelier and landed expertly on Reception.

"Did you see that, you ol' pair of puke-faced pus-buckets?" Granny Snott shouted to wherever Mr Nobody and Mr Crawley were hiding. But there was no reply.

"Hello?" said Mrs Odd. "Mr Nobody? Are you there?"

After a few moments, Mr Nobody scootled in through the hotel door.

"Sorry about that," said Mr Nobody, smirking. "We had a bit of trouble getting out of the sewer. Hope we didn't miss anything. Now, are you ready to impress me, Mrs Odd?"

Chapter Eight

PEDAL TO THE MEDDLE

That night, Mrs Odd went home feeling pretty mad. Edgar and Elsie were still miserable from Mr Nobody's comments on their less-than-brilliant pranks, but when they heard that he had missed Mrs Odd's altogether, they went even madder than their mother.

"That's just not fair!" said Edgar, swinging around the living-room lamp in frustration.

"He did it on purpose, I bet," said Elsie, sliding up and down the banister.

"I don't see the point in carrying on," said Granny Snott. "He's going to fail us whatever we do."

"Perhaps," said Mrs Odd, "but we have to keep trying. Where's your father?"

"He's upstairs," said Edgar, "hanging upside down from the curtain rail."

"He thinks he's a bat today," said Elsie, stifling a little giggle.

"Oh, great!" said Granny Snott. "One minute he can't remember who he is, the next he thinks he's a bat?"

"It's going to take time for his memory to come back," said Edgar.

"Well, it's his turn for inspection tomorrow," said Mrs Odd worriedly. "How is he going to manage when he can't even remember who he is?"

"Leave it to us, Mum," said Elsie.

"How are you two going to help?" asked Granny Snott. "You promised you'd look after my cart!"

"I know," said Edgar. "And we will. You just keep Dad locked away here where he can't do any damage, and we'll do the rest. We'll take care of ol' Nobby..."

The next day, Edgar and Elsie found themselves living most child Meddlers' dream – operating their very own Pedlar Meddler cart full of goodies and baddies and tricks and treats. Granny Snott had given them full Pedlar Meddler powers of instant magic and travel while they were in control of the cart.

Pedlar Meddlers rarely ever meet together

in a Meddlers' Marketplace – that would attract too much attention. Instead, they wait for a Meddler to call for them. Just like Meddlers get The Shudders when a prank is about to fail or go horribly wrong, a Pedlar Meddler can tell if they are being called upon and where to go.

Edgar and Elsie had had a rather busy morning's work and were doing a quick stock-check when they got their next call.

"Do you think we have enough Snapping Yo-Yos?" asked Elsie.

"I think so," said Edgar. "But we're running low on Elastic Bogey Bands. We're running low on quite a lot of stuff, actually. We're pretty good at selling this Pedlar Meddler stuff!"

Suddenly they both felt their ears and toes tingle.

"Number 13 Rotten Row?" said the twins at the same time.

"But that's where I live," said Edgar.

"I know," said Elsie. "I live there, too."

They leaped on to the cart. Elsie pulled the

small green lever that made the Atomic Jet Boosters emerge from the compartment beneath the cart's wooden handles. Edgar pressed the big red button that ignited them and then...

WHOOOOOSH!!!

Off they flew like a pair of freaky fireworks, Edgar in the driving seat (sitting cross-legged on top of the merchandise) and Elsie clinging on for dear life, her legs flailing behind her. The world became a blur as Edgar steered them wildly across roads and pavements, over hedges and postboxes, narrowly missing pedestrians who had absolutely no idea what that whoooooshing sound was that they had just heard.

In no time at all, they landed at Number 13 Rotten Row. Quickly, they screeched to a halt in their back garden.

"Wow..." said Edgar, his hair standing on end. "What a rush that was!"

103

"I know..." said Elsie, her pigtails still twirling like twin propellers. "And why are we here? Where's our customer?"

At that moment, they heard a rude noise.

"What was that?" asked Edgar.

"It sounded like a rude noise," answered Elsie.

"Where did it come from?" asked Edgar, looking around.

"It was that bush," said Elsie, pointing to a small, grotty little bush that grew in a lonely corner of the Odds' back garden.

"Bushes can't make rude noises," said Edgar.

"They can if they're raspberry bushes," said Elsie.

"Stop that delightful wordplay at once!" It was Mr Nobody! His beaky nose was peeping out of the bush. "It's me! I called you here, it's an emergency!"

Edgar rolled under the small bush, while Elsie did a triple backwards somersault. In the centre of the bush, Mr Nobody was sitting, drumming his fingers menacingly.

"Why are you two operating as Pedlar Meddlers?" he asked.

"It's Granny Snott's cart," said Edgar. "She said we could look after it cos she's helping out at home."

"Ah yes ... your dad," said Mr Nobody, smirking as he wrote something down in a very important file. Edgar and Elsie looked at each other with a burning hatred for ol' Nobby.

"You called for our assistance?" asked Edgar.

"Yes," said Mr Nobody. "I have a very serious problem and I need your help..."

"Ooh, what?" asked Elsie, a little too eagerly.

Mr Nobody took a deep breath. "I've ... run out of ... paperclips..." Mr Nobody put his head in his hands and breathed deeply.

"Paperclips?" said Elsie with a smile. "You've come to the right place – we've got LOADS of paperclips. What kind were you after?"

"Just your standard paperclip, please," said Mr Nobody. "And please keep your voice down. I can't have anyone hearing that. I ... never mind.

Just give me whatever you have."

"Well," Elsie took a deep breath, "we've got folding paperclips, trick paperclips, breakaway paperclips, miniature paperclips, giant novelty paperclips, solid gold paperclips, paper paperclips and staples."

"Just some normal, everyday paperclips will be fine!" Mr Nobody hissed.

"Everyday paperclips?" said Elsie. "I don't think we've got any of those, have we, Edgar?"

"Tell you what, Mr Nobody," said Edgar, "why don't you check around the back here with Elsie to see if you can see any. You've got a dodgy wheel on your desk, I'll just take a look ... see if I can fix it." He bent down and fiddled with the wheel.

"Dodgy wheel?" Mr Nobody got up from his spinny chair and crouched down to where Edgar was looking. "Hmmm, now you come to mention it, my desk has been veering slightly to the left lately. See what you can do."

Edgar reached into his meddling pockets and

began tinkering with Mr Nobody's desk, as Elsie and Mr Nobody scanned Granny Snott's cart for paperclips.

"Ah, here we go!" said Elsie. "Exploding paperclips. Will these be OK?"

"No!" Mr Nobody huffed. "For the last time, I don't want to prank anybody with them. I just need them to keep my papers in order! That is the very nature of a paperclip: to clip paper!"

"Oh!" Elsie smacked her forehead. "Why didn't you just say so? I've got loads of paperclips right here." She reached into her own meddling pockets, and pulled out around three hundred and eighty-one paperclips and thrust them into Mr Nobody's hand.

"At last!" cried Mr Nobody. "Paperclips! How I have missed ye!"

"Are you about done down there, Edgar?" Elsie snuck a look at her brother as he was stashing his tools back into his meddling pockets.

"All done, Mr Nobody." Edgar grinned and shot a wink at Elsie. "That wheel should be as good as new."

"Well." Mr Nobody sat back down behind his desk. "At least you've managed to do something right. It's just a shame there are no boxes to tick on my form for 'wheel fixing' or 'paperclip vending', so none of this counts towards your inspection in any way."

Edgar and Elsie smiled at Mr Nobody from behind the cart like little angels.

"That's OK, Mr Nobody, sir," said Elsie.

"We were happy to help," said Edgar.

"Good," said Mr Nobody. "Now, I have to get on with inspecting your father. Where is he? Inside, I trust, babbling like a bald baboon?"

"Of course not!" said Edgar in mock shock, shooting a look to Elsie. Mr Odd was inside, of course, and he was actually babbling, but more like a hairy gibbon than a bald baboon. The last thing Edgar and Elsie wanted was for Mr Nobody to go inside and start bothering Mr Odd in the state he was in. "Dad's right here with us!" Edgar continued. "He's hiding in one of the cart cupboards, planning a very special surprise prank for later on."

"Is that so?" said Mr Nobody suspiciously.

"Knock on the door and hear for yourself," said Edgar.

Mr Nobody crouched down and knocked on the side of the cart. "Hello? Mr Odd? Are you in there?"

There was another knocking sound and Mr Odd's voice replied, "Aye, I'm in 'ere, and I'd appreciate a bit of peace and quiet. I'm plannin' and plottin'..."

"I see," said Mr Nobody. "And what exactly are you planning and plotting?"

"Ah..." said Mr Odd's voice, "that's fer me to know and you not to know until I says you can know..."

"I see," said Mr Nobody, who didn't. "Well, maybe I'll just head back to the house then and inspect the filth levels of your cockroach infestation. Toodle-oo." Mr Nobody pushed his makeshift office over to the front door, whistling as he went.

"That went well," said Edgar.

"Very well," said Elsie. "Between us we made it sound exactly like Dad was knocking on a door and speaking when really he was doing neither!

So what were you doing
all that time behind the
desk?" Elsie asked.

"I'll tell you later,"
grinned Edgar.

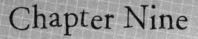

Chapter Nine

BRIDAL SHOWER

Edgar and Elsie walked into Number 13 Rotten Row at the same time as Mrs Odd and Granny Snott arrived back. As soon as they entered, they found something rather peculiar taking place.

"What's going on here?" Mrs Odd asked a passing flower-boy.

"It's a wedding, that's what," said the boy.

"A wedding!" Edgar spluttered. "In our house?"

It was!

There was all sorts of weddingy stuff being set up: banners strewn hither and thither, and balloons strung up thither and whither.

Feeling bemused, Mrs Odd and Granny Snott made their way through the house to the back garden where even more weddingified stuff was going on.

"I don't believe it," said Granny Snott. "Here in the back garden, even more weddingified stuff is going on!"

"What is going on here?" asked Mr Nobody, who had just arrived at that moment with Mr Crawley.

"A wedding, apparently!" said Edgar.

"A wedding?" screeched Mr Nobody. "In a Meddling household? Crawley, bring my entire office outside, I want to make sure I put all of this in my inspection report..."

Mr Crawly pootled inside, bowing as he did so and transferred Mr Nobody's office from the Odds' living room to the back garden.

"Look! It's that awful Mrs McSimmons," said

Elsie, nodding in the direction of the awful Mrs McSimmons. "What's she doing here?"

"Having her wedding in our house by the looks of things," Edgar helpfully pointed out.

"Why in the name of The Great Meddler What Lives in the Sky is Mrs McSimmons having her wedding at our house?" said Mrs Odd.

She marched up to Mrs McSimmons and tapped her on the shoulder. "Excuse me!" she said in her very best we-did-not-agree-to-host-a-wedding-in-our-house voice. "We didn't agree to host a wedding in our house."

"Oh," said Mrs McSimmons, "but I'm afraid you did. Mr Odd himself rang me and said I could have the wedding here, as the church has been flooded."

"The church has been flooded?" said Mrs Odd, Edgar, Elsie, Granny Snott and Bob, the Odds' dog, all at the same time (it was one of the stock sentences they practised weekly on their speaking-in-unison evenings).

"Yes," spluttered Mrs McSimmons, "with custard, would you believe?"

The Odds looked at each other.

"Flooded with custard, did you say?" asked Mrs Odd.

"That's one of Dad's favourite pranks," said Elsie.

"But why would Dad then offer to have the wedding *here*?" asked Edgar.

"He's just plain loco in his coco," said Granny Snott.

"Or someone else flooded the church with custard and he genuinely thinks he's a wedding planner," said Mrs Odd. "Look, there he is organizing the wedding guests into rows according to size!"

"This just can't happen!" Elsie whispered. "Mrs McSimmons is the horrible, borriblest, no-good-immoriblest person who ever lived!"

"It doesn't matter about all that now," Mr Nobody chimed in, "as I think I've seen enough of your pranking expertise to pass judgement on you all! And I have to say, I wouldn't get too comfortable here – there's no way I'm going to be able to pass you. You'll be pranking the old folks at the Trott Old Folks' Farm before the day is done!"

"Oh no! Whatever will we do?" said the Odds in unison.

"Hang on a chicken-stuffing minute!" said Granny Snott, stalling for time. "Now that there's going to be a wedding here, can't you at least hold off on writing your report until it's over?"

"Very well," said Mr Nobody, putting his pen and notepad away. "I suppose I can prolong your agony for a little while."

"Please don't!" said the groom.

"Are we ready to begin?" said the vicar, who was sitting at a huge, rusty pipe organ that had clearly been rescued from the church.

Everybody sat down, except for Mr Odd, who was now juggling five purple umbrellas whilst riding a unicycle.

"If we Meddlers host a wedding at our house, we'll be laughed out of the Meddling community!" Elsie whispered to her family.

"She's right," said Edgar. "How are we going to get out of this one?"

"I don't know!" Mrs Odd shouted back in her quietest whisper. "Is there anything on Granny Snott's cart that can help us?"

"All we've got left is half a rubber chicken and a second-hand large-print owl dictionary, third edition," said Edgar.

"We've had a busy day," added Elsie.

"Before we begin the ceremony," the vicar began, "we shall sing hymn number four hundred and twenty-two and three quarters: My Soul is a Happy Little Sea Lion."

"We've only got to the end of this ceremony until Mr Nobody fails us!" Edgar squealed.

"Brollies up, everyone!" Mr Odd skipped along past Edgar, Elsie and Mrs Odd, handing out umbrellas. "It looks like rain to me."

"Dad!" said Elsie. "Not now, we need to think of something, and quick!"

"Brollies up, everyone! It looks like rain to me!"

"Oh, do stop blathering on, you ape," Granny Snott snapped. "I haven't even got one!"

"Brollies up, everyone! It looks like rain to me!"

"EDGAR! Now is not the time for your impressions!"

"Brollies up, everyone! It looks like rain to me!"

"EDGARRRR!"

"That wasn't me that time!" said Edgar, in his dad's voice.

"Oh, for the love of giant millipedes, let's just put the umbrellas up," said Mrs Odd.

"Shall we all stand to sing," said the vicar, who had spent his time thus far warming up each and every one of his fingers from the tip to the bit above the knuckle.

The congregation rose, hymn books open at hymn number 422¾. The Odds and Granny Snott stood cowering at the back, umbrellas raised and brains thinking faster than a downhill cheetah on roller-skates.

The vicar planted his thoroughly warm fingers on the keys of his pipe organ. A muffled squish-a-rific sound could be heard. The congregation looked up just in time, as approximately fourteen gallons of royal grade Festering Putridness shot out of the organ's pipes and landed with a

SQUELCHAROO!!

... covering everyone from head to toe. Everyone! Mrs McSimmons, the flower-boy and the vicar. But none were more covered than Mr Nobody, who had at that moment chosen to sit on his desk to get a better view of the wedding.

"What was that?" asked Mrs Odd.

"What is this?" asked Edgar.

"Why didn't I get an umbrella?" asked Granny Snott.

"My wedding dress!" screeched Mrs McSimmons, who leaped, screaming, and jumped over the Odds' garden wall. "I can't let the groom see me like this!"

With a creak and crack and fiddle-de-dee, the Odds' back gate broke open and every wedding guest was washed away. Granny Snott and Messrs Nobody and Crawley were the only ones left soaking in Festering Putridness, stinking like a Dog-Poo Collectors' Convention on the hottest day of the year during an air-conditioning repairmen strike.

"Well…" Mr Nobody said, dripping in filth and fungus. "I have never … EVER known a family as — "

"Clever as this, Nobby?" said Mr Odd, leaping on to a table of Festeringly Putridmungous sausage rolls like a hero, then promptly slipping off again and spoiling the effect. "You have to admit it was the best prank EVER! It was I, Mr Odd. I flooded the church with custard. I contacted manky old Mrs McSimmons and told her to have the wedding here. I made sure all my family had umbrellas (except for you, you carnivorous old carbuncle)." He looked at Granny Snott. "It is I that have been pranking you, ol' Nobby-chops, since the very moment you walked through my door and that dustbin lid prumpled me on my nit-carrier. Did you really think I'd gone bat-bananas from being knocked unconscious? HA! I had you good and proper, didn't I? It was all a crafty little sneak to buy me some time till I could think of the best prank ever and – wouldn't you know it – Mrs Muck-Simmons fell right into my arms. Though not literally, of course – she'd break them right off. "

Everyone fell silent.

"What?" said the little Odds in unison.

"What?" said Mr Crawley.

"By the golden nose hair of The Great Meddler What Lives in the Sky..." said Mr Nobody, who was having a hard time processing it all.

"I can't believe it..." said Mrs Odd. "All this time ... all along you were ... fine...?"

"We've all been so worried about you, Dad," said Edgar.

"I haven't..." mumbled Granny Snott.

"We all thought you'd lost your mind," said Elsie.

"I can't believe you've put us through all this," Mrs Odd sniffed. "It's ... brilliant, my little in-growing hair! You fooled us all! And what an end result! What a prank!"

"It wasn't enough for me to see a dustbin lid full of Putridness on your head," said Mr Odd, leaping down from the table of Festeringly Putridmungous sausage rolls and slipping once again. "I had to do more than we did when we were young Meddlers, otherwise you'd be sure to fail us. I'm not one to hold a grudge, but I've thought about that every single day at least once every half-hour for the last twenty-four or so years. And now, it gives me great pleasure to say ... gotcher."

The entire Odd family began to whoop and holler, like it was a national holler-day. Edgar and Elsie jumped on the back of their warthogs and galloped around the garden wall. Mrs Odd was doing backflips among the blueberries and Granny Snott was dancing a Meddler's jig with gusto.

"Well..." Mr Nobody looked as though he had swallowed a spiky cannonball. "I don't know what to... I was just doing my..."

"Job?" said Mr Odd. "Since when did your job include surprise inspections done in person? Admit it, Nobs, you may have done all right in your meddling career, Head Pranker and all, but I've done all right, too. I gots me a meddlesome old wife and two tiny troublemakers who think I'm the best prankster in the world. All this time I've been jealous of you, but I reckon you were actually the one who was jealous of me."

Mr Nobody looked angry. His face swelled to several times its usual size and went through all the shades of red there are, as well as some new recently discovered ones.

"You're right!" he burst out after several minutes of swelling and shading. "Mrs Odd was my secret love, you see, but you were the one she picked. You have her, and I, Nobody, have nobody."

Mrs Odd let out a gasp.

"You've got me, oh King of the Creepy Crooksters..." said Mr Crawley.

"Oh, what use are you!" said Mr Nobody. "You weren't even aware I'd run out of paperclips!"

Mr Crawley gasped. "You ... you ran out of paperclips?"

"Yes," said Mr Nobody. "I had to get some from those two." He pointed a snobby finger at Edgar and Elsie.

"Well, well, well." Mr Crawley began to stroll up and down Mr Nobody's desk. "According to Meddling Law subsection one, paragraph three, as set down by Prime Meddler, Mr Mopp, three hundred years ago: 'A Head Pranker must never run out of paperclips and if he does, he then forfeits the right to his Head Prankership.'"

Mr Nobody's face turned as white as a sheet.

"I ... er ... I didn't ... I wasn't..."

"Don't feel too bad," said Edgar. "I took your paperclips."

"Aha!" screeched Mr Nobody. "But that in itself is in direct contradiction to Meddling Law. Don't nick from other nickers!"

"Aha," grinned Elsie, "but we gave the same ones back to you, so it's not technically nicking. Pretty good, eh?"

"Plus," said Edgar, "we're only Trainee Tricksters. We didn't know about that law..."

"You ... measly little maggot-chompers!" Mr Nobody spat. "How could you!"

"It was easy," said Edgar.

"I'll have you all for this!" Mr Nobody was even angrier. "You'll never meddle in this town, or any other, ever again."

"I'm afraid they will, Nobby," said Mr Crawley.

"Don't you call me Nobby!" said Mr Nobody. "I hired you as my assistant because you're a massive creep. Creepy Crawley, they all call you!"

"Indeed," said Mr Crawley. "But I'm not your assistant any more. You allowed yourself to be pranked by two Trainee Tricksters and even though they didn't realize it, your lack of paperclips makes you fired. And what with Mr Odd's spectacular prank, it means that the Odds' will pass their inspection."

Mr Nobody slumped on his chair behind his fancy old desk. "Fired ... I can't be fired!"

"Oh, then let us fire YOU," said Edgar, pulling a concealed lever on Mr Nobody's desk, which made two Atomic Jet Boosters appear underneath.

"It'll be our pleasure," said Elsie, pressing the red button on a remote control she got out of her pocket. "Bye-bye now."

The Atomic Jet Boosters ignited with an almighty whoosh and Mr Nobody, his desk and his fancy, fancy spinny chair shot up into the sky like a meddling firework...

Chapter Ten

ODDS WELL THAT ENDS WELL

"He's gone!" Mr Crawley cheered and began dancing for joy, which was awful as he couldn't dance at all.

Mr Odd put a hand on Edgar and Elsie's shoulders. "Now that was an excellent piece of meddling, my little dung beetles."

"I installed the boosters when he called on us to replace his paperclips," Edgar explained.

"Not bad at all," said Granny Snott. "I feel sorry for your victims when you become Professional

Pranksters if you're pulling this standard of prank when you're only Trainee Tricksters."

Mr Crawley, as a temporary stand-in for Mr Nobody, who was now orbiting the Earth, started to write up the report.

After he had left, the Odds and Bob retired to the living room for a good old cup of nettle juice and some peace and quiet after a hectic few days.

"I can't believe you pretended to have lost your mind, Dad," said Edgar, full of admiration for his dad and full of sausage rolls that he had mostly scraped clean of Festering Putridness.

"You certainly fooled us all," said Mrs Odd.

"You're a real wonder, Dad," said Elsie.

"You could've got me an umbrella, too," said Granny Snott, who was sitting in a bath by the fireplace.

"It was a struggle," said Mr Odd, "but it was worth it to finally get even with ol' Nobby."

"We should have known you were pranking us when Mrs McSimmons said the church had been flooded with custard," said Mrs Odd.

"Ah yes," Mr Odd smiled smugly. "Me and my spare custard nozzle had a fun time out on the ol' town that night, I can tell you."

The Odds grinned.

"What did you do with all the furniture and stuff?" asked Edgar.

"I brought it all home," said Mr Odd. "It's here – in the living room – right now – along with the male-voice choir. You're actually sitting in a font!"

"Oh yeah," said Edgar, looking around, "I wondered what all these pews and candles were."

"Well, I'd better be off," said Granny Snott. "It's been a real treat pranking with you all. Except for you, you drip-nosed dog-wart."

"I'll miss you, too," said Mr Odd.

The Odds waved Granny Snott a fond farewell as she went outside and rocketed away on her cart to have adventures of her own.

"What a day!" said Mrs Odd.

"What a day indeed!" said Mr Odd.

"Indeed what a day it was today!" said Elsie.

"What are we going to do with this   male-voice choir?" said Edgar.

"Good question," said Mr Odd. "Why don't you tour the country doing thrash-metal songs in a choral style?"

"Good idea!" said one of the singers. "Come on, gang, let's get out of this dump."

"That was a low blow, calling my house a

dump!" said Mr Odd as the choir left.

"I can't believe you was pranking Mr Nobody all along, my little itchy, flaky scalp," said Mrs Odd, turning to her husband.

"Yeah, Dad," said Edgar, "you're my hero!"

"Best of all, Mrs McSimmons got the pranking of a lifetime!" said Elsie.

"And to celebrate," said Edgar, "let's race about on our warthogs!"

"Brilliant idea, son!" said Mr Odd. "We'll race to Loch Trott and back again. Last one here has to take a bath!"

"Great!" said Elsie.

And the Odds galloped around on warty warthogs until the cows came home. Then they galloped around on them, too.

The
Odds

Adam Perrott

Have you ever fallen flat on your face
when you're carrying an ice cream?
Or put down a drink, gone back to get
it and it's nowhere to be seen?

That's the Odds at work! A family of
Professional Pranksters who delight in
playing the most rib-tickling tricks on
the townspeople of Trott. But when
the fiendish Mr and Mrs Plopwell move
in nearby, the Odds meet their match.
This calls for some serious
mischief-making...

GRANNY SNOTT'S PEDLAR MEDDLER TEST QUESTIONS

Being a Pedlar Meddler is a fine occupation for any aspiring Professional Prankster, and one that goes back centuries, if not hundreds of years. Below are a series of questions that will determine if a career as a Pedlar Meddler is right for you.

1. What is the quickest way to get to your next customer?
A. A straight line.
B. Take your time, they're not going anywhere.
C. Rocket boosters. Obviously.

2. You are given the wrong change by a customer who has already started to walk away. Do you:
A. Forget it – you've got lots of things to sell.
B. Explain to them kindly and politely that there's been a mistake.
C. Strap them to the back of your cart, ignite the boosters and take a few turns around the block until they cough up the money *and* their breakfast.

3. You catch a thief pilfering goods from your cart. Do you:

A. Let them go. After all, Meddlers will be Meddlers.
B. Inform the proper authorities that a Meddling Law has been broken. Never nick from other nickers!
C. Strap them to the back of your cart, ignite the boosters and take a few turns around the block until they cough up the money *and* their lunch.

4. Your cart breaks down on the way to a customer. Do you:

A. Forget it. Not your problem.
B. Send another Pedlar Meddler in your place.
C. Fix your cart as quickly as possible. A good Pedlar Meddler knows the mechanics of their cart inside out.

5. A rival Pedlar Meddler has been selling on your patch to your regular customers. Do you:

A. Ask them nicely over a cup of hot chocolate and some shortbread if they wouldn't mind letting you have your regulars back.
B. Run them over the next time you see them. After all, you've got a living to make.
C. Strap them to the back of your cart, ignite the boosters and take a few turns around the block until they cough up the money and their tea.

RESULTS

MAINLY As — It looks like the life of a Pedlar Meddler is not for you. Never mind. Buy a fishing rod, sit in someone's garden and contemplate a career as a garden gnome instead.

MAINLY Bs — Not too shabby. You may have the makings of a Pedlar Meddler after all, but you're probably not ready for your own cart yet.

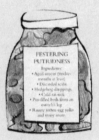

FESTERING
PUTRIDNESS

Ingredients:
• Aged mucus (twelve months at least)
• Discarded scabs
• Hedgehog droppings
• Cold rat-sick
• Pus-filled fresh from an ostrich leg
• Runny rotten egg yolks and more more

MAINLY Cs — CONGRATULATIONS! You possess all the requirements necessary to become a fully fledged Pedlar Meddler. Or, indeed, a member of staff at any high street retailer.